John Italia
The Birds of the Harbor

Pictures by Elena Caravela

Shenanigan Books

Text copyright © 2006 by John Italia

Illustrations copyright © 2006 by Elena Caravela

The artwork is rendered in pastels.

Library of Congress Control Number: 2006920019
ISBN: 0-9726614-7-6

Printed in China

For Mary – SI

For Tom, Vaughn, and Julian,
all masters in the sharing of inner most music–EG

The Birds of the Harbor

called down the winds of autumn. And the boy who loved to watch them fly answered them in his heart.

Sometimes he imagined they heard him and gave him the power to speak the language of birds. Then, in words as clear and beautiful as were ever heard, he was able speak what was hidden in his heart.

Now his mother was becoming worried, for she had seen him go down to the harbor day after day to talk to the birds. And as she had been warned by her own mother, she said, "Don't you know that the birds of the harbor are very mysterious and that if you try to discover their secrets, they shall come to build a nest in your hair?"

"That is just a story," argued the boy, refusing to be frightened.

"It is not a story!" his mother cried. "If I hear that you have been to the harbor again, you will get the spanking you deserve!"

But the boy was stubborn.

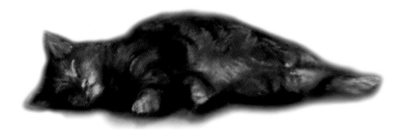

One day as he was by the harbor watching the birds, he grew very sleepy. He looked up to the sky and said, "My friends, I would like nothing better than to listen to you all day, but as you can see I am very tired...."

He was about to say a great deal more, but he found himself yawning so much that he lay down on a tuft of grass. There he dreamed that he had the voice of the birds and that he could say whatever was most dear to him in the most beautiful words imaginable.

When he awoke much later, his neck felt very heavy and there was a strange rustling noise in his hair. As he climbed to his feet, a seagull sailed down from high above and seemed to land right on top of his head.

Slowly, he raised his hands, first to his shoulders, then to his neck and finally to his head. How astonished and frightened he was to find that a nest of seaweed had been woven right into his hair.

"Oh, what will I do?" he cried. "How can I go home with a bird's nest on my head? Now I will be punished for sure!"

"Hello," said the seagull, peeking out of his nest and looking down at the boy.

"I can understand the birds!" gasped the boy, so overcome with joy that he forgot his fear. "Now I will be able to say whatever is most dear to me in the most beautiful words imaginable."

But the seagull looked down from his nest and sang:

A swirl of seaweed for my bed
a crown of seashells on my head
simple treasures given me
at harbor's sandy edge

I scorn the books the wise men read
these winds shall be my books instead
they whisper tales of things to be
and words of truth unsaid

Farewell the dream that must have fled
farewell the life I would have led
for the things that are most dear to me
can never be sung or said

At this the boy grew sad again. "You mean," he said, "that even the birds are unable to speak of the things that are most dear to them?"

"Too true, too true," replied the seagull. "Forgive me, but I must go now, for I have business to attend to with the other seagulls. In the meantime, see to it that you take good care of the egg I have laid in the nest...for it is a magic egg and if you throw it into the ocean in three days time, you shall have any wish that you desire."

And the bird flew off.

When the boy returned home and his mother saw that he not only had a bird's nest on his head, but a bird's nest with a little spotted egg in it, she became so upset that she began to cry.

So she sent him to bed without his supper.

The next day as he walked to school, people laughed and pointed at the him, saying, "See what good all your time at the harbor has done? You have a bird's nest made of seaweed on your head!"

At school they teased him more, and someone even drew him into a fight. But the boy was careful to lay his little egg aside so that when he fought, the egg was not damaged.

The next day was no better. How glad he was when the third day came and it was time to go to the harbor. There, he threw the egg into the sea where it fell to the bottom and was swallowed by a great fish, who swam to the surface and asked, "What is your wish?"

The boy wished for the wisdom of the birds, who could sing so sweetly and cry so loudly, though they too were unable to speak the things most dear to them.

"Your wish is granted," said the fish, who then sank to the depths of the sea.

When he returned home, his mother and all the people of the town gathered around him, for they saw that the bird's nest was gone from his head and they wondered how it had come about.

But the boy did not answer. Instead, he just sang:

Farewell the dream that must have fled
farewell the life I would have led
for the things that are most dear to me
can never be sung or said.

The people were puzzled and did not know what to make of it. But the boy was very happy and his mother was very proud. And before long, the story was known far and wide, for the boy's voice was so sweet and his song so beautiful that even the birds of the harbor came to hear him sing.

...for the things that are most dear to me can never be sung or said.